COVID-19

AFRICA AND BEYOND

A collection of English Poetry

COPYRIGHTS
P. PALEMO MARKETING T/A
DZEKANYI PUBLICATIONS
P/A BIRIIRI CHIMANIMANI
ZIMBABWE

COVID -19 Africa and Beyond

ISBN NUMBER 978-1-77924-202-0

Email: naapenyai@gmail.com
Tel: 0772 332 645 | 0712 948 959

CONTENTS

MASK UP ZIMBABWE

Live - before you leave

Love - before you leave

Live – before you leave

Live and lead a legacy

Live and leave a legacy

A vibrant legacy.

Mask up Zimbabwe

Mask up every Zimbabwean

Mask up for Zimbabwe

Mask up for Africa

Live well beyond Africa

Live well for one Africa

I love you Africa I love you

I love you

I love you

I love you Africa.

Mask up for the future of Africa

Africa is beautiful

Africa is very very beautiful

Africa is me

Africa is you

Africa is all of us

Let's all live for each other

Live for one another in Africa

Mask up for the beauty of Africa

Mask up for the benefit of Africa

Mask up beyond the beauty of
Africa

I love you I love you Africa

I love this Africa

I love my Africa

I love my continent of Africa

Mask up beyond the contents of
Africa

I love you I love you

My love is for Africa

Go away covid-19

Go away out of Africa

Africa my Africa

Africa beyond generations to come

Generate a generous generation of Africa

A united Africa

Is an exciting Africa.

Passion is key,

Be passionate about Africa.

Patience is key,

Be patient about Africa

Patriotism is very important

Patriotism was brewed here in
Africa

Patriotism is brewed here in Africa,

I love you I love you Africa

I love you I love you

I love you Africa

Africa free from the virus

Africa free from covid – 19

Bye bye bye bye covid -19

Bye bye bye bye – go away.

Prayer is prosperity

Prayer is everything

I am here now - praying for Africa

You are there now- praying for
Africa

We are here now – praying for
Africa

I love you I love you I love you

I love you daughter of Africa

I love you son of the soil

Son of the soil of Africa

I love you – once more Africa

I love you forever more Africa.

Pray for our motherland Africa

Peace is our priority

Let there be peace before
prosperity

Let there be light – after covid – 19

Let there be sunlight – after covid-
19

Let's all live to light up Africa

Africa is light

Let's light up our Africa

Let's all light up beyond Africa

I love you I love you I love youuuu

I love you – Africa.

One man with light

Will light up Africa

One man with light

Will light up the majority.

The majority is you

The majority is me

That majority is us.

I love you I love you Africa

I love you beyond this pandemic

I loved you before this pandemic

And I swear to love you.

I love you I love you.

Saka reshuka rakapera

nge – teaspoon,

Anganai edu ana – Teaspoon?

Anganai edu ane – teaspoon?

Teaspoon for Zimbabwe

Teaspoon for Africa

Teaspoon for the village

Teaspoon for the global village,

Covid-19 is a global pandemic

Listen to the echoes of the
pandemic.

Mask up each and everyday

Mask up from Biriiri to Beitbridge

Mask up from Durban to the

Diaspora ,

Zvichapora – zvichapera –

zvichapora

Mask up even in the Diaspora

Mask up from Chirinda to Chikore

Mask up from Chipinge to

Chimanimani

Chiendambuya right up to China

Mask up from Zvimba to Vhimba

Practice social distance everyday

Stay at home and stay safe

Don't mingle for no reason

I love you I love you Zimbabwe

I love you I love you

I love you Zimbabwe

Zimbabwe begins with you

Zimbabwe begins with me here

Zimbabwe begins with us here

I love you I love you –

Zimbabweans

I love you Zimbabweans

Live to see the future

Live to work for the future –

Nyika imovakwa – nevene vayo

Ndiwe iwewe mwene wayo

Ndini inini mwene wayo

Isu isusu vene vayo.

Vene vayo – today

Vene vayo – tomorrow

Vene vayo – at sunrise

Vene vayo – at sunset

Vene vayo – just before dawn,

Live to build your beautiful country

Your beautiful country – Zimbabwe

Your beautiful people –
Zimbabweans.

Zimbabwe my Zimbabwe,

I love my Zimbabwe

Zimbabwe my beautiful Zimbabwe

Zimbabwe my united Zimbabwe

Zimbabwe my patriotic
Zimbabweans

I love you Zimbabwe – mncwaaa!

I love you Zimbawe beyond –
mncwaaa!

Mask up – kupfuure mombe –

Dzaive pachikoforo nezuro,

Mask up – kudarika Bhoferi na
Bhokirandi

Mask up Bhuruwayo –

Mask haina kuti bhuru

Mask haina ubhururu

Mask haina kuti mukuru

Kana kuti muzukuru

Kana kuti muzaya watsekuru

Mask up nawo swo tsekuru

Mask up beyond doubt

Une nzee dzekuzwa ngaazwe nyamashi

Asante sana – Zimbabwe

Aluta continua – beyond covid-19

Zimbabwe must live – beyond this pandemic

Africa has to survive –

Beyond this wave in transit.

Aluta continua – Zimbabwe

Aluta continua – Africa

Aluta continua our global village

Aluta continua – every human
being

Be passionate about your precious
life

Be passionate about today

Be passionate beyond tomorrow

Be prayerful – beyond tomorrow

The future is fuming with everything

The future is you

Be passionate about yourself

Be passionate about your
surroundings

Your environment –

The trees and the mountains

Preserve all those trees

Live beyond the mountains

and the trees

Live beyond covid-19

Live beyond love and laughter

Live beyond peace and unity

The unity of your country and Africa

The patriotism of your country and Africa

Africa I love you

Africa I do love you

I love you I love you I love you

I love you the countries of Africa

I love you beyond measure

Africa is prayer

Live beyond your prayers

Aluta continua your prayers

Aluta continua our profound prayers –

Mutsvurangoko munamato wako

Mutsvurangoko munamato wangu.

Africa is harmony

Lets all live in harmony.

Africa is the living future

Lets all look to the future.

I love you I love you

I love you - my fearless future.

FACEMASK THE FACE OF AFRICA

Africa face mask week 23-30 November 2020

It's not over

Until it is over.

Facemask your face today

Facemask the face of Africa today.

Facemask the face of Ghana

Facemask the face of Gambia

Mask up Zimbabwe, Zambia and Zanzibar

Mask up the beautiful face

And handsome face of Africa.

Mask up one face of Africa

Mask up that cultural face of Africa

Complacency is the mother of failure,

Procrastination is the road to poverty,

Facemask the face from poverty

Facemask your face from the virus

Prosperity begins from your mind,

Facemask your mind

And have the correct mindset,

Success is a sound mindset,

Get set for a good mindset.

Facemask your face of profound prosperity

Africa is a land of overflowing prosperity.

Facemask that face full of prosperity.

Covid-19 must comes first

on your priority,

Our continental priority.

Facemask your face –

Little boys and girls

Big boys and girls

Facemask your face-

ladies and gentlemen.

Facemask your face -

All walks of Africa

Facemask our continent of Africa.

Our Africa of yesterday

Our Africa of today

Our profound Africa beyond

tomorrow.

Facemask your face-

Until this pandemic is over.

It's not over

Until it is over .

Complacency kills

Procrastination will kill

all of us here

from presidency to pedestrian

covid-19 knows no age, race, class

color, nationality, profession or
status.

It knows no pride,

It will kill you and your pride

It will kill you and your ignorance

It will swipe us all

When we ignore rules and
regulations.

Our Africa of today

Our Africa forever Amen.

Its not over – dear Africa

Its not yet over

My dear African sisters

And big brothers.

Respect all protocols

Of this marauding pandemic.

Put all systems in place

Retain your beauty in place

Beautiful girls will always -

wear face masks every day ,

Until the pandemic is over.

Women of great resilience

Will never say “no”

to face mask.

It’s not over

Until it is over.

Corona virus is here

for a while,

if not forever

Let’s live life

the new normal way.

Covid-19 has known no race

Black or white-

It still colors you the same.

It's hear to paint everyone

With the same old brush.

Facemask your face –

Your beautiful face - of Africa

Facemask your face –

You handsome face of Africa

Facemask your face

Your unique face of Africa.

Corona virus knows -

no handsome face.

Covid-19 knows no ugly face,

Facemask your aspiring ugly face,

From the ugly face of covid-19.

Facemask your Christian face

And retain your Christian face.

Facemask your beer face

And if possible – avoid beer.

Avoid covid-19 beer please!

Avoid covid-19 women

Avoid covid-19 prostitution.

Avoid men with money.

Covid-19 is also after men

With plenty money

Women with lots of money.

Covid-19 is also after women –

Without any manners

Live with your exceptional

manners.

Money and covid-19

Makes you cough.

Corona virus

knows no country

Corona virus

knows no continent

Corona virus

knows no argument.

It might be too late

For a late argument.

Avoid taking a late .

Live your one life with love.

Live your precious life

With passion, patience and prosperity

We are all here to live once.

We are all here for a purpose,

Live to serve your purpose.

Live to serve yourself

Live to serve others

Life is good with others

Life is good

with father and mother

life is so full of fun

with families and friends.

Live beyond your families and friends

Life is so nice as a nation,

Let's all live as one nation.

Live beyond your country and continent

Live beyond Zimbabwe and Africa

Love you Africa – love you

I love you I love you I love you.

I love you my village

I love you beyond my village

And my global village.

I love you I love you I love you.

I love you my global village.

I love you I love you,

I love you all in my local village.

I love you I love you,

I love you everyone on this global village.

Life goes beyond this global village.

The vaccine is here today

Get vaccinated Africa.

I love you Africa

Especially when you are
vaccinated.

Vaccine is the way to go

Vaccination is a global vision

Vaccination is the current
conqueror

Don't be immune to the vaccine

Vaccine is the way forward.

Let's all move forward with the
vaccine.

Let's all move forward

With vaccination program.

Vaccination is progress

I believe in progress

I believe in people with progress

I believe in people with passion –

Passion for your one life.

I believe in patience and
perseverance

Let's be patient with the virus.

Let's be a patient to the virus,

We are here to conquer the virus

Live life the new normal

Live your life with profound hope.

This is a phase,

It will one day pass away

Please – don’t pass away

Before this phase passes away.

Live life the new normal.

This new normal is inevitable

Don’t be impossible.

Be yourself and defeat the virus.

Victory is certain in everyday,

It's only when you don't quit.

Quitters don't win

Game changers always win.

Quitters never win

Please don't quit

And join the game changers

For everything with a beginning

There is an end,

Life itself is not endless.

Look forward to everyday

Look forward to life everyday,

Look forward to a new normal
everyday.

Victory is inevitable everyday

Your eyes on the prize everyday

Your conscience on the price
everyday.

Your eyes on Christ everyday

There is everything in Christ
everyday.

There is everything in you-
everyday

There is something in place

For you – everyday.

Look up to tomorrow – everyday.

Live up to yourself – everyday

Live up to yourself-

Beyond yourself everyday.

Facemask your surviving face

Facemask all the way

Facemask to survive.

Social distance for survival

Sanitize to chase away Satan

Covid-19 is as good as Satan

Sanitize this additional Satan,

From Zambezi to Limpopo

That's our face of Zimbabwe,

From Cape to Cairo–

That's our living face of Africa

Facemask this face of Africa

Facemask the wealth of Africa

Facemask the culture of Africa.

Love you Africa.

Love you love you – love you,

The face of our living Africa.

The darkest hour

is nearer to dawn

get this message

my dear daughter.

Live to see

this profound dawn.

Carelessness

will caress your life

Carelessness

will caress all of us here.

Carelessness will kill

all of us here.

Let's all live with care

and conscience.

Respect the virus

And it will respect you in return.

Respect all rules and regulations

Respect the law

And not the policeman.

The policeman is part and parcel

Of the law in place.

Wear your mask for yourself

Wear your mask

Not for the law

Neither for the law maker

Neither for the policeman.

Wear your mask,

Not for the mass.

He who has ears-

Let him listen

to these words.

He who has eyes

Let him see,

The world is living at a crossroad

Crossroad with the virus

Crossroad with chaos from the virus

Real chaos from this pandemic.

Your health

is your greatest wealth today

respect your health.

My health

is my greatest wealth

beyond tomorrow.

Your health

is our African wealth

Asante Sana - African wealth

Bholato bholato our wealth.

Bholato bholato –

Africa week of face mask.

Facemask

The vital face of Africa.

Bholato bholato – Africa

Bholato bholato -

face of Africa.

Asante sana Africa

Aluta continua Africa.

Face of Africa is me

Face of Africa is me today

Face of Africa is you

Face of Africa is you - today.

Face of Africa

is all of us in Africa.

Let's all face Africa - with passion

Let's all face Africa

With an African perspective.

Africa free from diseases

Africa with a healthy

health delivery system

let's put our health systems in
place

Preserve our Africa

Preserve our AFRICAN face today,

It takes two to tackle

It takes two to tango

It takes two to Zimbabwe

It takes two to Africa

You and I makes Africa.

Come let's make Africa

Let's make Africa tick everyday

Let's make this Africa great

From our great people.

There is a life to live

After covid-19

Let's all live beyond covid-19

Preserving your African face -

Is my African mission today.

My African agenda,

Let's all join hands

on this mission.

A mission to accomplish,

Let's all live to accomplish.

Preserve that face

Of a precious continent.

My dear brothers

And shinning sisters,

Africa is the two of us

Let's move the two of us

Beyond the virus.

Let's all move – beyond the virus.

Move them – beyond the virus.

Move everybody – beyond the virus

Come everybody – beyond this
pandemic.

Africa is a story teller

Let's all live

To tell a story

The story of corona virus.

The history of the facemask

Asante Sana

face of AFRICA.

Aluta continua Africa

Aluta Continua – face of Africa

Aluta continua - the beauty of
Africa

Black is Beautiful

Black is brilliant

Black is brains

Black is never behind

Let's live the virus behind.

Behind the face of Africa

Behind the face of poverty.

Africa of prosperity

We live to conquer

One day at a time

One prosperity at a time

Let’s thrive to live beyond covid-19

Let’s move forward in prosperity

Forward in faith

Forward in confidence

Forward without failure -

With the virus.

We all live to conquer everyday,

let’s conquer the virus

Victory is beyond the virus.

The new normal

it's here today.

This new normal

It's there tomorrow morning,

Let's all stop moaning

Before tomorrow morning,

Comply and abide

by contemporary regulations.

To wear your face mask

is the new normal.

Let's facemask

The wealth of Africa.

It all begins with a facemask.

It all begins with you

And none other.

Social distancing

is the new normal.

Regular hand washing

is our new normal.

Staying at home

is the way to go.

Warambe kupangwa

Haasi Panganai,

Warambe kupangwa

Haana mipango iri gumi ,

The ten commandments.

Covid-19

is an abnormal pandemic

Stay away stay away

I will repeat this again –

Stay away stay at home.

Stay away stay away,

from this abnormal pandemic.

It is not over

Until it is over.

Facemask Africa today

Facemask the face of Africa.

Facemask and save Africa.

Pride carries no prosperity

Pride does not pay

Pride will never wake up

and pay anyone.

Lets not get carried away

With our personal pride.

Leave pride behind every history.

Wear your mask –

not your pride.

Emotions will never

Get us into motion.

Lies will never

Leave us in love.

If we can stop lying

We can start loving.

Love does not lie

Real love does not lie

Real live has to be lived,

Corona virus is a real life

We are living this life –

It's not a lie.

We are all sailing

Through this pandemic,

This is true to life,

We cannot dispute this.

Don't dispute

the disciplines of covid-19.

Covid-19 is real

It's not a manufactured lie

It's not a cooked lie

Like beer that we brew,

Like food that we cook

Let's all live life

With covid-19 in mind

Mind the virus.

Don’t say – I don’t mind

Don’t say – I don’t care

Don’t say – it’s not my baby

Whose baby is it then?

Don’t say – it doesn’t matter,

Life matters

Nobody wishes to die today

Or either tomorrow morning.

Nobody wishes to moan

Neither tomorrow morning.

We all live with a mission,

Look after your mission statement,

Your health is your mission
statement

Choose life

Leave the virus alone

Leave the pandemic alone

Stay away from the virus.

Always remind yourself –

I have a life to live.

It's not over

Until death do us part.

It's not over

Until it's over .

Wash your hands –

including your pride.

wash your hands –

inclusive of your brain.

Just like crime-

Pride does not pay,

What pays off

is to wear your mask.

Don't get carried away

along the way

Covid-19 will carry us all -

Beyond our living imaginations

Beyond our living expectations.

Swallow your pride

and remain vigilant.

It is not over

Until it is over.

Wear your facemask

Wear your original mindset

Wear your beauty

and your brains,

If you want to remain

Bright and beautiful.

Wear your correct attitude –

If you want to reach your altitude.

Wear your destiny

Before you wear out

Before you go down,

Wear your Ubuntu

And go down with Ubuntu,

Umuntu ngumuntu ngobuntu.

Wear Ubuntu – wherever you are

Wear Ubuntu – where ever you are

Wear exceptional Ubuntu .

In your everyday walk of life.

Life is derived from Ubuntu.

Life is lived by abantu

Life is lived by umuntu

Umuntu ngumuntu ngabantu.

Africa revolves around umuntu

Halala halala African umuntu.

Halala halala abantu beAfrica

Halala halala African Ubuntu.

Halala halala

Our African history and culture,

our beautiful Africa.

Halala halala !

our beautiful Africa

halala halala !

our African beauty,

black is beautiful

black has always been beautiful

black will always be beautiful.

Preserve the beauty of Africa

Wear your mask with pride

Wear your mask

With confidence conniving -

With you.

Halala halala !

our African culture.

Halala halala!

Our culture beyond culture.

Our culture beyond measure.

Its not over

Until you start

washing your hands

Don't touch MEN

(Mouth – Ear - & Nose)

Lockdown

Before you are locked up

In a prison cell,

I hate Mandikise prison cell

I hate death and it's ingredients

Covid-19 is one of it's ingredients.

I hate Hwahwa prison

I hate Hwahwa

I have since stopped

drinking Hwahwa.

Lockdown today

And experience the new normal

That's prevailing

on the global village.

Lockdown

and save your one life.

Live life the new normal way

Live life with

new rules and regulations.

Covid-19

is full of contemporary rules

and regulations.

Life itself

is full of rules

and regulations,

Fools look down

upon rules and regulations.

Fools despise

wisdom and instructions,

the Bible tells us so.

Lockdown

to the prescribed regulations

Lockdown

for the sake of Africa

Lockdown –

For this beauty of Africa

Lockdown for you and me.

It takes two to tango

It takes two to tackle

Rise up and tackle Africa

Rise up

and raise Africa.

Rise up

And raise everyone.

Rise up and raise someone

I have raised someone

Out there.

Raise someone out there today

I have raised somebody

Out there today,

Rise up

and raise someone today.

Rise up

and raise your families.

I rose and raised families

Families with appreciation

And families with depreciations.

Rise up and rise beyond measure

Rise up and rise and raise your community

Rise up and rise and raise your country

Rise up beyond your country

There is Africa – beyond your country

There is the global village

Beyond your village

Rise up beyond your global village.

Rise up

and raise others.

You fall

When you allow others –

to fall. .

You rise –

When you allow others –

to rise.

You rise

through blessing others.

Rise up and bless others.

Rise up and bless someone,

Pass your blessings

Before you pass away.

Heaven and earth

Shall pass away.

Rise up

and bless your neighbor.

Rise up and keep praying

You rise -

through your prayers.

You rise

Through your passionate prayers.

Rise up

and pray every morning.

Rise up and pray

Whilst you are busy rising.

Christ strengthens you everyday

I can do all things -

Through Christ

who strengthens me.

Facemask your face –

Through Christ

who strengthens you.

I facemask my face-

Through Christ

who gives me

enough strength.

Strength to carry on

Strength to live on

And leave yesterday behind

The old has passed away

The new normal is here.

Rise up

With the new normal.

The new normal

Has raised new people

New businesses

And new business people

New business personalities

New game changers

Be a new game changer

Under the umbrella

of a new normal.

Rise up

and raise Africa.

Don't catch your fish

And sell your own fish.

Don't sell fish-

Jesus was the foundation

of all parables.

I speak in parables.
Africa is the home
Of all parables.
We parade everyday
In new parables.
We swim in new parables
We even dine ad dance in new parables

Africa is the platform
of all folktales

Let's all live

to tell all folktales

covid-19.forktales.

Africa is the source

Of all beautiful cultures

Lets all live

to tell our culture

Live to respect your culture.

Live to respect your languages,

If you are Japanese –

speak Japanese.

If you are Ndebele –

speak pure Ndebele

If you are Xhosa –

speak Xhosa.

If you are Tonga –

speak Tonga.

If you are Tswana –

speak Tswana

If you are Ndau-

rekete Chindau

Ndauwe ndauwe Chikore
neChirinda.

Africa is the mother

of all languages

Live to respect –

ALL languages.

Lockdown – lockdown

From Presidency to pedestrian

Preside over all rules

and regulations of Covid-19.

Lockdown to the prescribed

regulations.

Africa can hear –

He who has ears

Let him hear,

The voice of one Africa.

The voice of covid-19

The voice of regulations-

Facemask your face

Facemask this face

one face of Africa today.

Africa has got eyes;

He who can see,

Can see Africa

With an African eye.

Let's all see Africa

With African scenic

Africa with African beauty

Africa with African perception

Africa with African pride

Africa with African wisdom

Africa with it's African ideology

Africa with it's own philosophy

Africa with African vision.

Let's all see Africa – beyond Africa

He who has got eyes,

Let him see the face of Africa

Let him see – the beautiful face of Africa

On this global pandemic today.

It has spared no race,

It's busy running

a pandemic race.

It has spared no one –

Not even the elite

Not even the enlightened

Not even the Pharisees,

Ukafarisa –

unoenda nacho

chiPharisee chakocho!

(If you get carried away –

You will be no more tomorrow.)

Africa is smart .

Be as smart as possible

And wear your smart mask

Each and every day.

You don't need the police

To police you every day.

You live alone

without the police.

You die alone

without the police,

Live life the new normal way

Live life the covid-19 way

Be your own policeman –

Your mindset is your policeman.

Your dear conscience

is your number one policeman

Talk to your mindset everyday

Talk to your mindset –

before you wake up,

Talk to your conscience

Before you get conscious.

Before you even go to bed

Sleep alongside

your conscience.

Talk to your attitude

Until you reach your altitude.

Walk your talk –

Each and every day.

Walk your talk

Yesterday and today.

Walk your profound talk –

Where ever you are today

And where ever

you go today.

Wear your mask

Where ever you are

And where ever you go.

Above all –

believe in God,

Where ever you are today

And where ever you go today

And wherever you go tomorrow.

And wherever you are tomorrow

Wisdom is everything
Solomon asked
for wisdom from God
And he got it
from a loving God.

Ask and it shall be
given unto you.
Knock
and it shall be opened
Specifically for you.
God's time
is the best time to knock.

Pray to God.

Pray and pray and pray

Pray and never cease to pray

Pray

until something happens.

Pray

Until something happens

today.

I say pray

Until something happens

tomorrow .

Pray

until covid-19

bids farewell to Africa

farewell to your village

in Chimanimani village.

Until it bids farewell

To our country Zimbabwe

Zimbabwe Zimbabwe Zimbabwe

My country of birth Zimbabwe

Your motherland Zimbabwe.

Pray today and everyday

Until covid-19

Bids Farewell

to the global village.

Covid-19 will certainly go,

Covid-19 has to go

It's a must to go

God's time

is the perfect time

God's time

is the way to go.

Go away covid-19-

That is my prayer.

Go away covid-19

This is my profound prayer.

Go away lockdown

Go away every level of lockdown.

Go away every level of the virus

Our eyes

on our prayers

Our eyes

on our fasting prayer

Our eyes on the prize,

Christ is our prize

He is right here

to clear all our crisis

There is no crisis

For those that

liveth in Christ.

It is not over –

Until it is over

Let's all keep

our hope alive.

Live with love

and laughter every day.

Don't forget to smile – everyday

A journey of a thousand smiles –

It begins with a single smile.

Get up with a smile every morning

And resist from moaning.

Remember –

Your health

Is your wealth.

Facemask your wealth.

Keep hope alive – Africa

Keep your faith

and fear all in parallel.

Faith is here

to move all your mountains

Faith is here

to move every mountain.

Faith alone

will move all

our mountains.

So many rivers to cross

With faith

we will cross them.

With faith

We have crossed most of them

With profound faith

We are going to cross

The last river.

So many bridges to cross

Covid-19 bridges

Together

we will cross them,

It all starts

With your mind and attitude

and your facemask.

Facemask your face

And get vaccinated.

The vaccine is here in Africa

Let's vaccinate the face of covid-19

Vaccinate the face of Africa.

Africa is today

Tomorrow is lived today

Today looks after tomorrow.

Vaccinate all the faces of Africa

Today – and not tomorrow.

Africa will be happy tomorrow

Africa must STOP moaning
tomorrow -

If not from today.

Africa was rich before today

The scramble for Africa was
yesterday.

The scramble was a human being,
sin.

A human error during an era.

We can't go back to yesterday

Africa is rich before tomorrow,

Let's labor beyond tomorrow.

Labor beyond covid-19

Facemask the engine of Africa

Facemask the wealth of Africa.

Fear keeps you away –

From your faith.

Forward in faith.

Fear keeps us away from success

Turn the tables for your success.

Turn the tables

Beyond your vision.

Turn the tables

Beyond your reach.

Backwards

belongs to cowards

Backwards

belongs to Lot's wife

Leave Lot's wife alone.

Don't live

your life alone,

don't leave

your life to some one else.

Live for others

and your Africa.

Live for yourself

And for your continent

Facemask

the lives of Africa.

I love you Africa

God save Africa

From this fatal pandemic.

Ishe komborera Africa

Mambo wangu

Izwaiwo kuchema kwe AFRICA

Facemask

your face of South Africa.

Facemask

your face of Ghana and Gabon

Facemask that face

of Zambia and Zimbabwe

Facemask that face

of Egypt and Ethiopia

Facemask the face

of our continent of Africa.

I love you Africa - love you

I miss you Africa –

missing you.

Covid-19 is real

and alive today

Listen to what is happening

in your local schools and colleges

Listen to the business community,

Covid-19 is there

in the business community.

Listen to what is happening in Sweden,

France ,Italy, China and Britain

And the United States of America,

Just to name a few countries.

Facemask this global village

Facemask your global village now.

Covid-19 is real

each and everyday

Read the newspapers

and listen to news

On international TV stations

Covid-19 has left

no stone unturned

Covid-19 has turned

All tables globally.

Be realistic

with your lifestyle

please don't lie

to your own conscience

Be realistic

with your conscience.

Stop drinking

covid-19 beer

From the covid-19 breweries.

Don’t go out

with covid-19 men

Don’t caress

covid-19 women

Carelessness

will caress you,

mark my words of wisdom.

Carelessness

will caress all of us.

Come down to earth

And live with mother earth.

Facemask – mask up

like yesterday –

before you live

this mother earth.

Victory is certain

on mother earth.

Victory was laid

already at Calvary

Believe in Calvary.

All our eyes on Calvary today.

It's not over Africa

Until it is over guys.

Wear your face mask

I say –

wear your covid-19 mask

properly

always cover

your nose and mouth.

Again and again I say –

wear your face mask,

If you don't want to wear it,

You will wear out - quickly.

Wear it

If you want to win it.

We are all playing to win

Winners never quit

Quitters never win,

We are warriors of covid-19

An egalitarian team of winners,

We are a winner of corona virus.

Stay alert everyday

Stay informed everyday

Mask up your face everyday

First thing first – Africa,

Facemask your face Africa

Facemask the face of Africa

Your health

is your wealth

my dear Africa.

Wash your hands

with soap all the times.

Sanitize each and every day –

If you want to remove Satan.

Sanitize your hands -

If you want to bid

Farewell to Satan

Farewell to covid-19.

I love You Africa-

Free from covid-19.

I love you Africa

In post covid-19 era.

I love you Africa-

Beyond

covid-19 pandemic.

Victory comes in phases

Let's all go

through all these phases.

Lockdown –

stay at home

and stay safe.

Maintain social distancing

where ever you go today

and wherever you are today.

Practice social distancing with covid-19

But not with your God.

You need your God

More than anything else

You need your passion for prayer

More than any other passion.

God's power

is the greatest power,

All our eyes

on the greatest power.

Good morning Africa

Victory will soon

greet us in Africa.

Victory is certain in Africa

Divine intervention

It's here in Africa

Divine intervention

will divide covid-19.

Asante Sana one Africa

Aluta Continua Africa

Bholato bholato Afica

Bholato bholato

My profound Africa

My contemporary Africa

Bholato bholato

Sons and daughters of Africa.

Aluta continua Africa,

Aluta continua our Africa.

Asante Sana Africa.

I LOVE YOU AFRICA

This is a message

from your motherland

to my fatherland-

I love you Africa

I love you

Love you.

I love you children of Africa.

I love you South Africa

I love your face

Beyond covid-19.

I love you

Beyond all these challenges.

Covid-19

is our contemporary challenge

I love you

beyond all these challenges.

Attitude is key

There is no altitude

Without attitude.

There is no quality

In quantity resolutions.

Lets all resolve

To stay at home

And stay alert.

Covid-19 is always alert

It’s never late to kill

It’s never late to destroy

It’s never late again

To look after yourself

I love you Africa

I love you South Africa

Love you love you.

I love you - Zimbabwe

I love your face

Beyond covid-19

I love you

Beyond post covid-19

Love you.

Let’s say this together –

I love my face

Beyond covid-19

Help me God

Save me God

Answer my prayers

As I pray today.

As I fast today

As I walk today

As I work today

During this covid-19 era.

I love my children

and grand children.

I love my father and mother

I love all my parents of Africa

Including all my global parents.

Save my village

Chimanimani village and beyond

Save my global village

Africa ,Europe and beyond.

Save all my relatives and friends

in the diaspora and beyond.

Save my mother and father

Out there in the diaspora

Save my family and my clan

My community and my country

And my global village.

Let there be light in Africa

Let there be light

In Africa and its countries.

I can't recite

all of them by names

But I can recite

all of them in one prayer.

Today I pray for you Africa

From Cape to Cairo

Caress all our aspirations

with love.

Guide us everyday

With our Christ like characters.

Let your will be done

Before ours.

Let your will be done

And let every tongue confess

That Jesus is Lord every day.

For every beginning

There is an end,

Let there be an end

To this fatal pandemic

Help us God

Help me God

Help us God.

Help us beyond covid-19

CHERISH THIS MOMENT

Tears translate into love

Loneliness into living love

Cherish this moment of love.

I fell in love

When I saw you

Moving together with love

I loved to fall in love

When I saw you

Drooping with love

Chose to love

And live with love.

I have chosen to lover you

Cherish this moment of love

Cherish to be in love

My tears translated into love

And I am hear to love

Cherish this love we have

Cherish this moment of love

That we have.

ATTENTION TO YOUR PASSION

Patience pays with time

Patience pays with passion

Pay attention to your passion

Pay attention to your patience

Pay attention to your pain

Before it pains you.

YOU NEED JESUS

When you are happy

As usual,

You need Jesus Christ

And live a crisis – free life.

When you are sad

And crippled with crisis

And you think you are miserable

You still need Jesus.

When you wake up

As early as usual

You still need Jesus

To wake you up

And put an abnormal smile

On your normal face.

You will need Jesus

In the aftermath

Of your afternoon

You nered Jesus

Even in the evening

Your need him more

During your sleep

Some slept

And they never woke up.

YEAR OF PLEASANT SURPRISES

Everything will be pleasant

It begins with a

pleasant surprise.

Pleasant year

Pleasant people

A pleasing God

Makes all things well.

I do have a pleasing God

A pleasing God is my God.

Asante sana – pleasing surprises

Aluta continua – my God.

www.ingramcontent.com/pod-product-compliance
Lightning Source LLC
LaVergne TN
LVHW012118170826
845678LV00014BA/2997

* 9 7 8 1 7 7 9 2 4 2 0 2 0 *